Plodney Creeper, Supersloth

Crabtree Publishing Company
www.crabtreebooks.com

PMB 16A, 350 Fifth Avenue,
Suite 3308,
New York, NY 10118

616 Welland Avenue,
St. Catharines, Ontario
Canada, L2M 5V6

Cataloging-in-Publication data is available at the Library of Congress

Published by Crabtree Publishing in 2006
First published in 2001 by Egmont Books Ltd.
Text copyright © Jane Clarke 2001
Illustrations © Cathy Gale 2001
The Author and Illustrator have asserted their moral rights.
Paperback ISBN 0-7787-0896-9
Reinforced Hardcover Binding ISBN 0-7787-0850-0

1 2 3 4 5 6 7 8 9 0 Printed in Italy 5 4 3 2 1 0 9 8 7 6

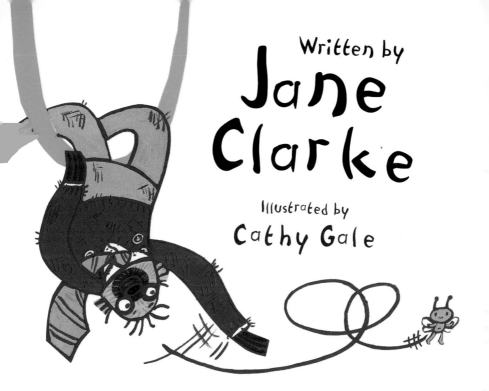

Written by
Jane Clarke

Illustrated by
Cathy Gale

Plodney Creeper, Supersloth

Blue Bananas

To Martin, Andrew, and Robert
with love
J.C.

To Dink Archer
C.G.

"Ye-hah!"

Plodney crashed through
the branches. A shower of
leaves fell on to the sloths below.

"I'm worried about Plodney,"
Mrs. Creeper said. "I think he might be
a bit . . ." She caught a leaf and chewed
it slowly. There was a faraway look
in her eyes.

On the branch above her, Plodney

stopped swinging. He held his breath.

"A bit what, dear?" Mrs. Clinger asked.

Mrs. Creeper lowered her voice.

"A bit . . . *fast*."

"*Fast*? Dearie me!" Mrs. Clinger said.

"A sloth should never be *fast*!"

"If only Plodney was as slow as Layzee," Mrs. Creeper sighed. "Look at her lovely green hair. Only the slowest sloths have green hair."

All this hanging around is making me sleepy.

"You're quite right, dear," Mrs. Clinger said. "My Layzee is very slow. She hardly ever moves. I am so proud of her."

Mrs. Creeper yawned and shut her eyes.

"I get tired just looking at Plodney," she said.

I can't help being **fast!**

Th-u-nk.

Plodney crashed down between them.

The branch swayed.

"Hello!" he grinned.

Mrs. Creeper and Mrs. Clinger

shuddered. Layzee opened one eye.

"Slow down, Plodney!"

"Oh Plodney," his
mother groaned,
"when will you learn to
hang around?"
"Don't worry, dear,"
Mrs. Clinger said.
"He'll learn to do that at
school, won't he?"

"Sorry, Mom."

It was dawn. The rainforest was waking
up. It rang with the calls of birds and
animals greeting the new day.
Only the sloths slept on.

Plodney swung up the creaky School

Branch. "Good morning, Mr. Gripper!"

"Early for school, again!" the principal

grumbled. "That's every day this week.

You must try harder to be late.

Remember Plodney, SLOTHS ARE

SLOW!"

Every morning Miss Snailspace's class

did Sleeping and Hanging Around.

They were all very good at it, except

for Plodney.

He did his best,

but it was no good.

Plodney could not keep still.

ye-hah!

"Plodney moved again!" Slo-Mo said.

"We should call him Speedy!"

"Or Flash," Layzee said.

The whole class laughed.

Plodney's wriggling!

He never stops!

Not like us!

At last it was playtime.

"Ye-hah!" Plodney yelled. He

grabbed a vine. "Let's play

Tarzan of the Jungle!"

Me, Tarzan!

"Only fast sloths like to play Tarzan of the Jungle," Layzee said. "We all want to play Dead Jaguars."

"That's right, Speedy!" Slo-Mo said.

"But we *always* play Dead Jaguars," complained Plodney.

"No we don't," said Layzee.

"Sometimes we play Statues."

"Plodney, you moved," Slo-Mo said.

He was the first one out as usual.

Layzee didn't move
for over three hours.
Layzee won.
"I'm the slowest sloth
in school," she boasted.

"It's not fair," Plodney told Miss
Snailspace. "I'll never be as slow as
Layzee."

"We can't all be as
slow as Layzee,"
Miss Snailspace
said.

After school Miss Snailspace had a word
with Plodney and his mother.

"I know Plodney finds it hard to slow
down, but he is doing his best," she said.

I must stay
still. I must
stay still.

"I am very happy to have him in my class. I think he is a super sloth."

Plodney felt very proud. Miss Snailspace thought he was a Supersloth! One day Plodney Creeper, "Supersloth" would show the world what he could do.

The next day, thunder rolled around the rainforest. The sloths were at school.

They were all doing Sleeping.

All but Plodney.

He was listening to the sounds

of the rainforest.

The birds were singing.

The monkeys were hooting.

The frogs were croaking.

They were enjoying the rain.

Cr-a-a-a-ck.

Suddenly, the sky lit up with a flash of

lightning.

"Wake up! Wake up!" Plodney shouted.

"School Branch has been hit!"

The sloths slept on.

They were very good at Sleeping.

It was their favorite subject.

Cr-e-e-e-ak.

This time the sloths woke
up. "School Branch is
breaking!" Plodney
yelled. "Use the
vines to swing
across to the trunk!"

"*Swing?* We've never done *Swinging*," Layzee said. "We're not all fast like you, you know."

27

"You can do it!" Plodney said. "Mr. Gripper and Miss Snailspace will swing across first and catch you."

Miss Snailspace looked nervously at Mr. Gripper. Mr. Gripper was trembling. Plodney handed them a vine.

28

"Ye-hah!" said Miss Snailspace weakly.

They landed in a tangled heap on the

tree trunk.

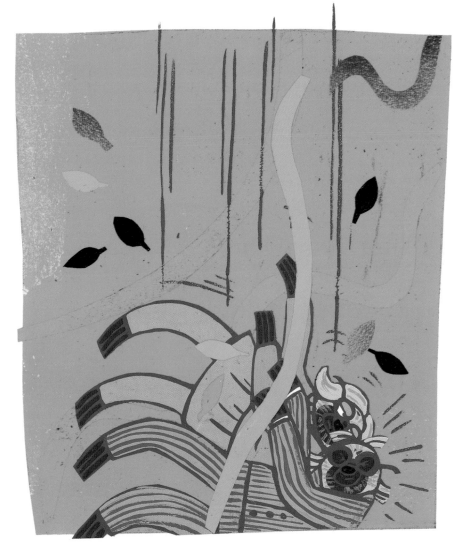

"Send them over!" Mr. Gripper

shouted. "Hurry up!"

The sloths looked at each other in

amazement. They had never heard Mr.

Gripper tell anyone to hurry up before.

Two at a time, the sloths swung

across to safety.

Mr. Gripper and Miss Snailspace caught

them as they landed on the trunk.

At last it was Plodney and Layzee's turn.

All the best vines had been used.

Plodney swung along the branch

to find a vine strong

enough for two.

Cr-e-e-a-a-ack.

School Branch gave way.

"Hang on, Layzee!" Plodney yelled.

School Branch dropped like a stone

toward the forest floor.

T-h-w-ack!

School Branch stopped falling. It was

caught in a tangle of vines.

Pop. Pop. Pop-pop-pop.

One by one, the vines broke.

"Hold tight!" yelled Plodney.

The end of School Branch hit the

forest floor with a cru-u-u-n-ch.

The leaves swished.

"Layzee! Are you okay?"

There was no sign of her. She must have lost her grip! She might be hurt. Plodney stood up and looked around. Where was she? He couldn't see anything. He couldn't hear anything. All the animals were still.

The rainforest was silent.

What was wrong?

There she was! Layzee lay on her back in the shadows of the trees.

"Are you okay?" Plodney called.

"I . . . I think so. I didn't fall far." Layzee tried to get to her feet but her arms and legs were too weak. She had been doing too much Hanging Around.

I can't move, Plodney.

Deep in the shadows, something stirred.

A dark shape slunk towards Layzee. Its

emerald green eyes glittered.

The jaguar crouched, ready to pounce.

Mmm,
a tasty sloth!
Easy prey...

Quick as a flash, Plodney ran towards

Layzee. The jaguar sprang.

Just in time, Plodney
pulled Layzee out of its
way. The jaguar hissed
with rage.

"Hang on to me!"
Plodney dragged
Layzee up the tree.

The jaguar leapt on to the branch beside them. It crouched low against the wood. Plodney grabbed a vine. "Ye-hah!" he yelled. The jaguar leapt after them. Plodney and Layzee swung across to another branch.

The jaguar lost its footing and fell to the forest floor. It circled the tree looking confused and limped away.

They got away! How strange.

"Phew," said Layzee. "I bet that jaguar was surprised to meet such a fast sloth!"

"Supersloths are always fast," Plodney said.

Plodney was having a great time.

They were playing a new game called Supersloth. They had to use vines to swing all the way around the tree.

The winner would be the first one back.

Today Plodney Creeper, "Supersloth," was going to win.

"Ye-hah!" Plodney yelled as he launched himself on to a vine.

"Ye-hah!" yelled Layzee, Dawdle, Hanga and Slo-Mo as they tried to keep up with him.

Slow down, Superplod.

He's the fastest!

And the greatest!

"It makes me tired just to look at them," Mrs. Creeper yawned.

"Me too, dear," Mrs. Clinger said.

"But we are all very grateful to Plodney. You must be so proud of him."

"I'm always proud of Plodney," said Mrs.

Creeper. She shut her eyes and smiled.

"He is a super sloth, you know."